FX 11-10

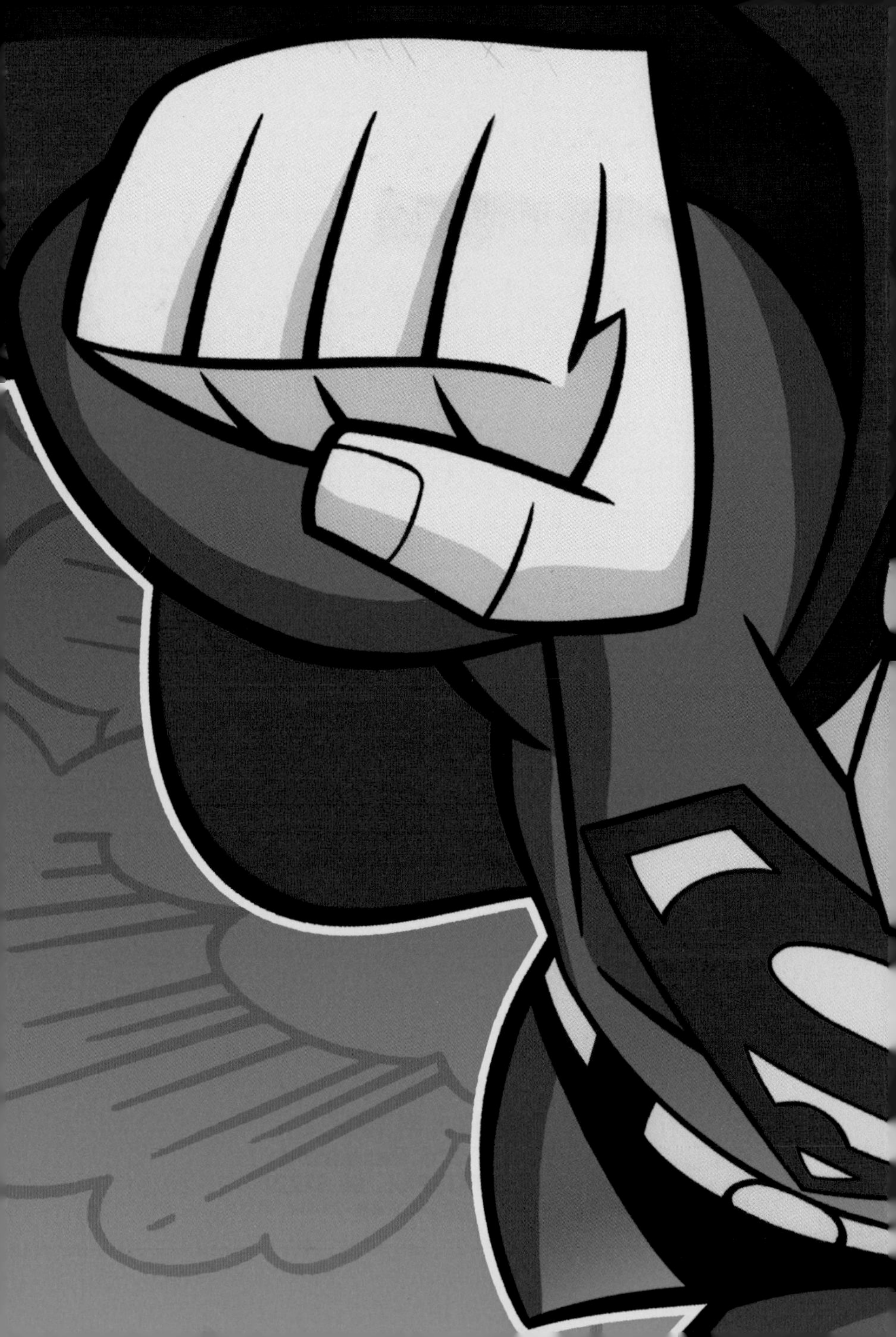

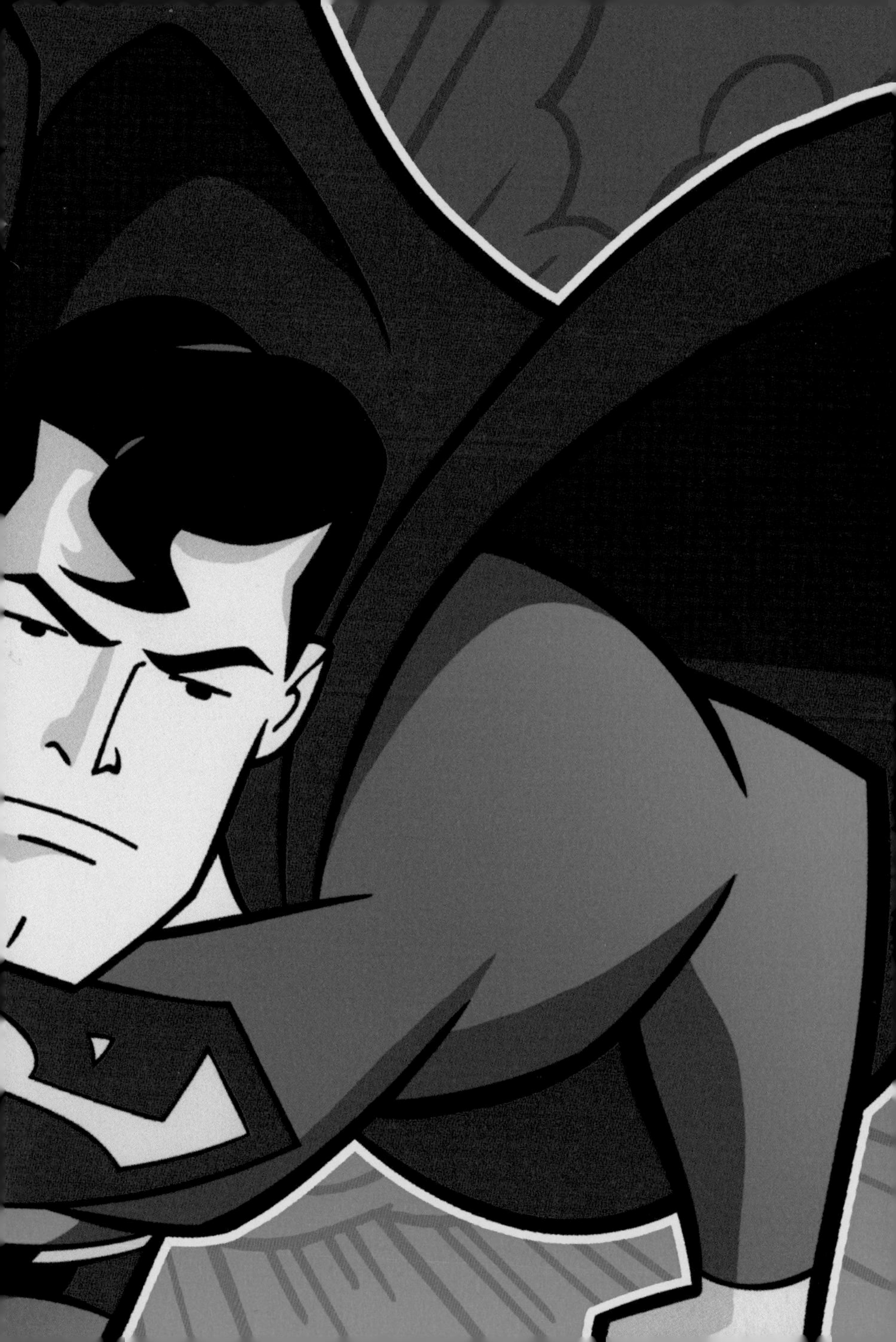

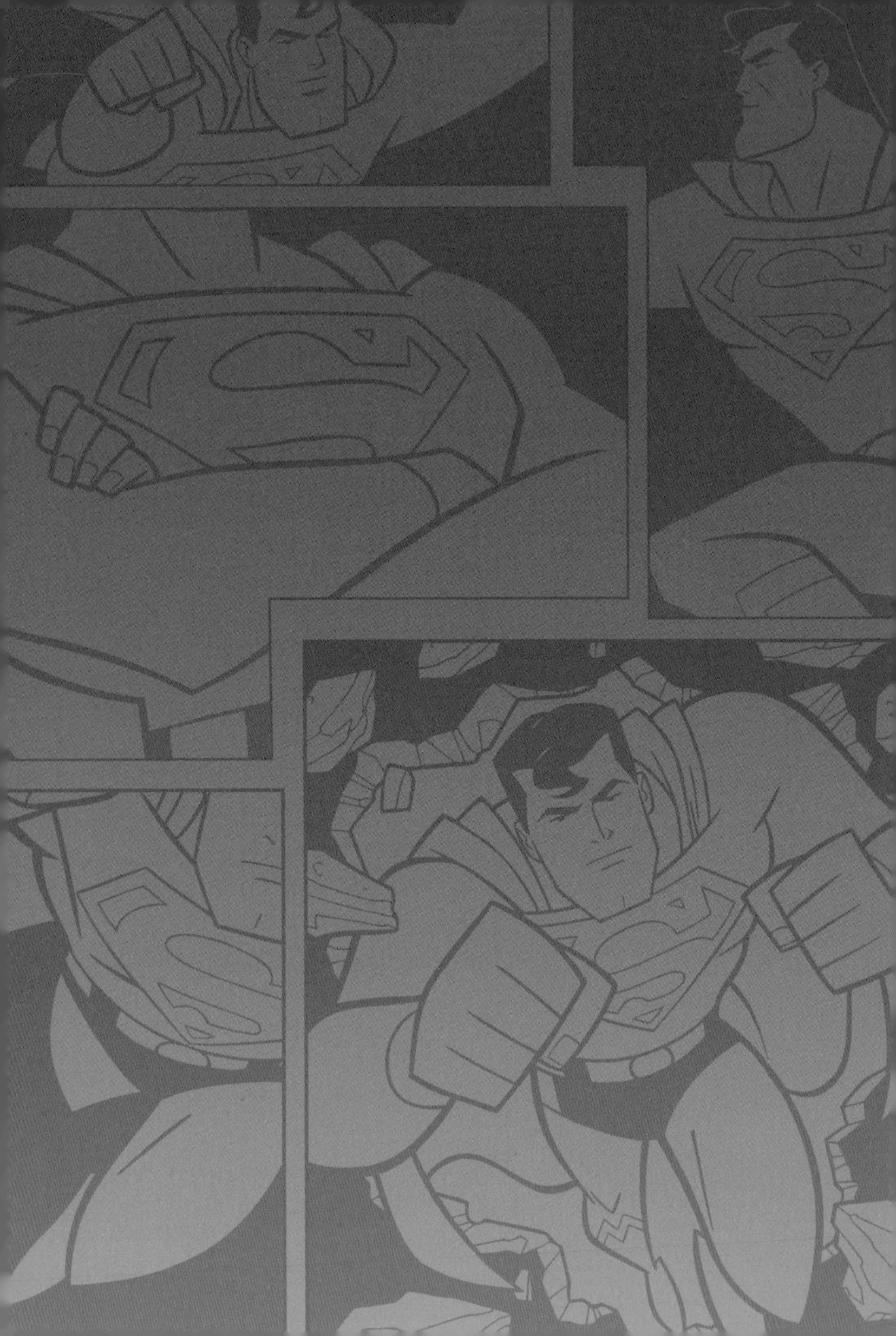

SUPER DC HEROES

SUPERMAN

THE DEADLY DREAM MACHINE

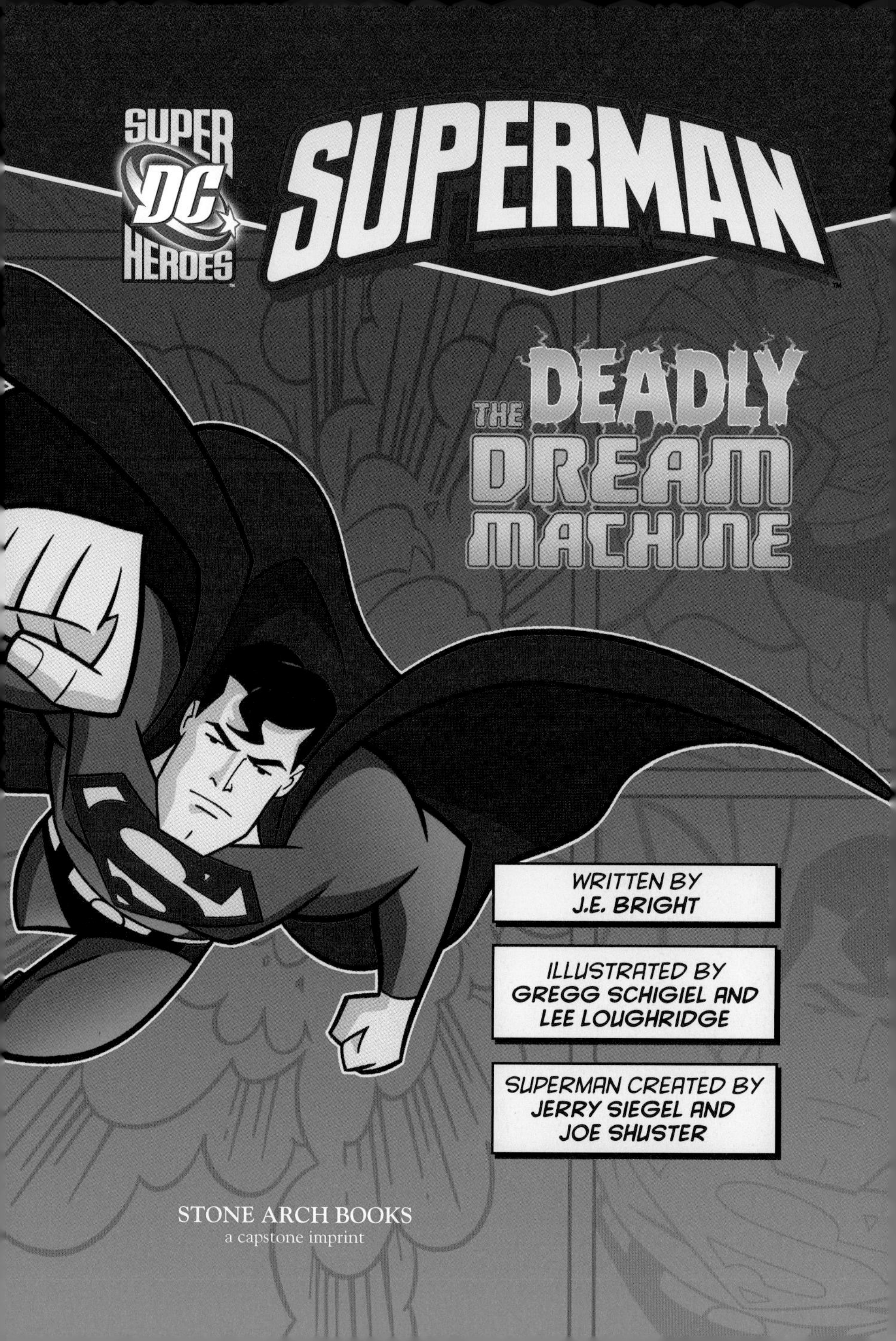

WRITTEN BY
J.E. BRIGHT

ILLUSTRATED BY
GREGG SCHIGIEL AND
LEE LOUGHRIDGE

SUPERMAN CREATED BY
JERRY SIEGEL AND
JOE SHUSTER

STONE ARCH BOOKS
a capstone imprint

Published by Stone Arch Books in 2011
A Capstone Imprint
151 Good Counsel Drive, P.O. Box 669
Mankato, Minnesota 56002
www.capstonepub.com

Cataloging-in-Publication Data is available at the Library of Congress
website.

ISBN: 978-1-4342-1978-7 (library binding)
ISBN: 978-1-4342-2759-1 (paperback)

Summary: Abra Kadabra, a super-villain from the 64th century, has
escaped from an alien prison and returned to Earth! Using a mind-control
machine, this futuristic felon hopes to brainwash the entire planet into
believing that he's the rightful ruler. To complete his evil plan, Abra
Kadabra has captured Superman, the only source of energy strong enough
to fuel his high-tech weapon. If the Man of Steel can't escape his dream-
like state and unplug himself from the mind-control machine, the world
will soon become a nightmare.

Art Director: Bob Lentz
Designer: Hilary Wacholz
Production Specialist: Michelle Biedscheid

Printed in the United States of America in Stevens Point, Wisconsin.
032010
005741WZF10

TABLE OF CONTENTS

CHAPTER 1

A DAY AT THE BEACH.....................................4

CHAPTER 2

UNBREAKABLE CHAINS...............................12

CHAPTER 3

POWER OF IMAGINATION..........................23

CHAPTER 4

DRAINING SUPERMAN 33

CHAPTER 5

SOLAR POWER..40

A DAY AT THE BEACH

Lois Lane put on her sunglasses and floppy hat. She relaxed into her lounge chair on the beach. "Ahh," she sighed happily, "this is the life, isn't it, Clark?"

"It's a beautiful beach, Lois," Clark Kent replied. He was lying on a lounge chair next to her, tilting his face into the bright sunshine. "It's very peaceful."

Clark and Lois were on vacation at a beach resort. There wasn't another person around as far as Clark could see down the sandy shoreline.

SPLASH! The only sound was the churn of the ocean waves. Behind them, past the sand covered with sawgrass, palm trees swayed in the breeze. Nearby, a tall, white hotel shimmered in the hazy heat.

The scenery should have helped Clark relax, but it had the opposite effect. He didn't feel right. Clark couldn't recall booking this vacation with Lois, or how they had gotten there. Clark had a strong feeling that he was supposed to be doing something important, but he couldn't remember. "I feel . . . strange," he told Lois. "Maybe it's *too* peaceful here."

"Don't be silly," Lois replied. She sat up, pulled out a bottle of water from her beach bag, and took a sip. "We both work so hard at the *Daily Planet*," she said, settling into her chair again. "We deserve a break."

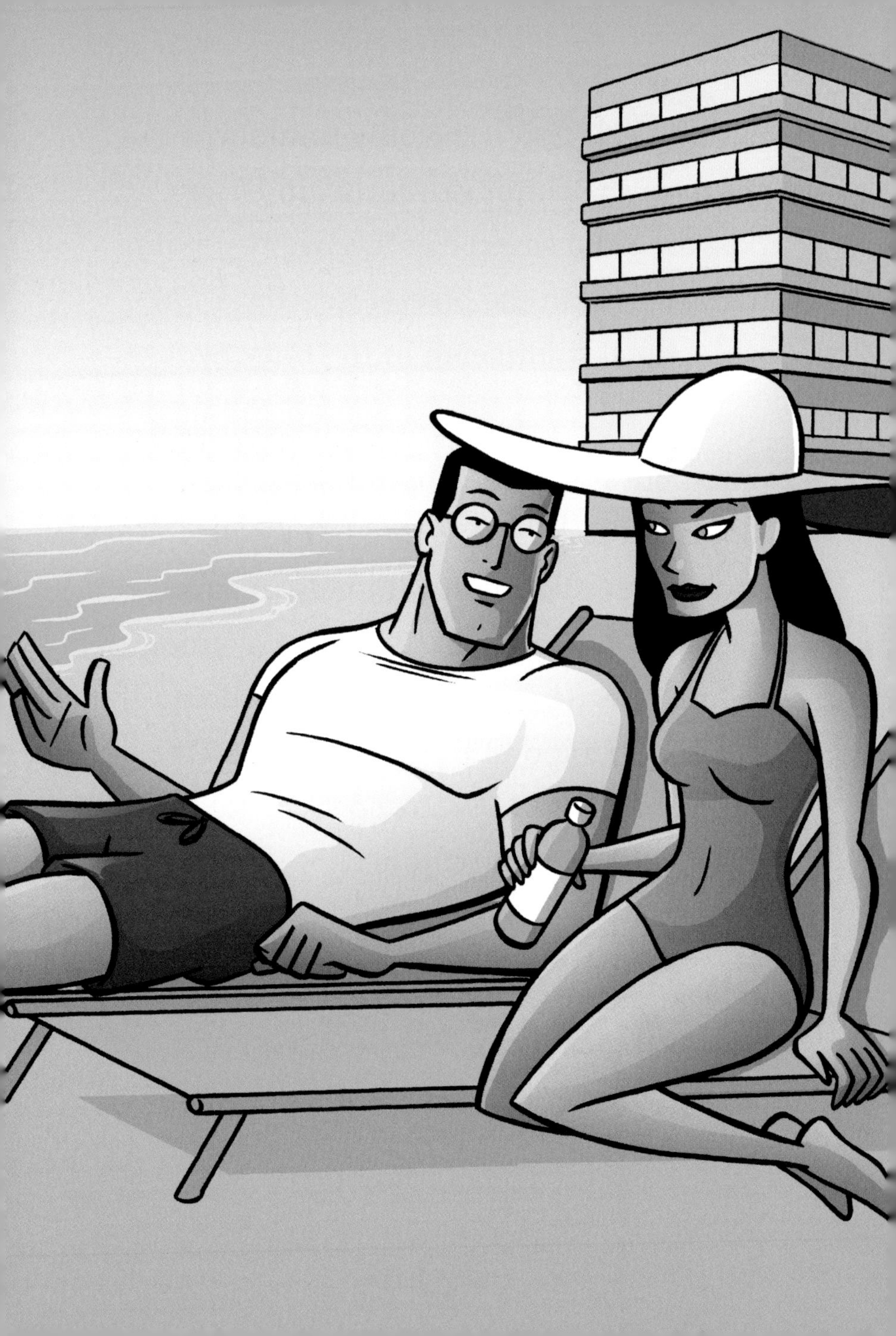

Clark glanced at her. "I thought you loved being a reporter," he asked.

"I do," Lois replied, "but I also deserve to relax now and then." She sat up and took off her floppy hat. "Let's go for a swim."

"Great idea, Lois," Clark replied. "The ocean does look inviting."

Together they hurried across the hot sand to the water.

Lois dived under a curling wave, but Clark waded into the ocean carefully. The water felt wonderfully cool.

For a while, Clark and Lois enjoyed playing in the surf. They jumped the ocean swells and bodysurfed the powerful waves. They even got into a splash fight. When Lois tossed a piece of seaweed that got stuck in Clark's hair, they both laughed.

"I'm getting tired, Clark," Lois said, heading back to her chair. "It's time to relax again."

Following closely behind, Clark suddenly realized that he had no idea when they had arrived at the resort. "I feel like we've been here forever," he told Lois. "How long has it been, anyway?"

Lois laughed. "What a funny thing to ask," she replied. "It doesn't really matter, does it? We needed a break. Just enjoy it."

"I'm trying," Clark said. "It just seems strange that I don't know what day it is."

"Forgetting about the real world is the best part of vacation," Lois answered, putting on her sunglasses. "We deserve it, especially since we just finished that big article on Superman."

Superman! Clark sat up straight. How could he have forgotten Superman? He *was* Superman. Mild-mannered reporter Clark Kent was just his secret identity. Something had to be terribly wrong if he couldn't even remember who he really was!

Suddenly, the beach around him shimmered. Lois looked transparent. He could see the palm trees right through her.

The beach resort wasn't real. This Lois Lane wasn't real. Clark realized that he wasn't really there.

Clark blinked his eyes, and the beach disappeared. He found himself lying on his back, dressed in his Superman uniform. The broiling sun beat down on him. All around Superman were huge pieces of high-tech equipment. He was on top of a smooth metal platform.

Superman struggled to sit up, but he was held down by massive metal handcuffs that hummed with power.

The sound of loud footsteps caught Superman's attention. He turned his head to look.

He immediately recognized the tall man on the other end of the platform as Abra Kadabra, a villain from the 64th century. **CLINK CLANK!** Abra Kadabra was tinkering with a computer panel on one side of a giant stack of mysterious technology. He didn't notice that Superman had awoken.

It was then that Superman remembered exactly how he'd ended up there.

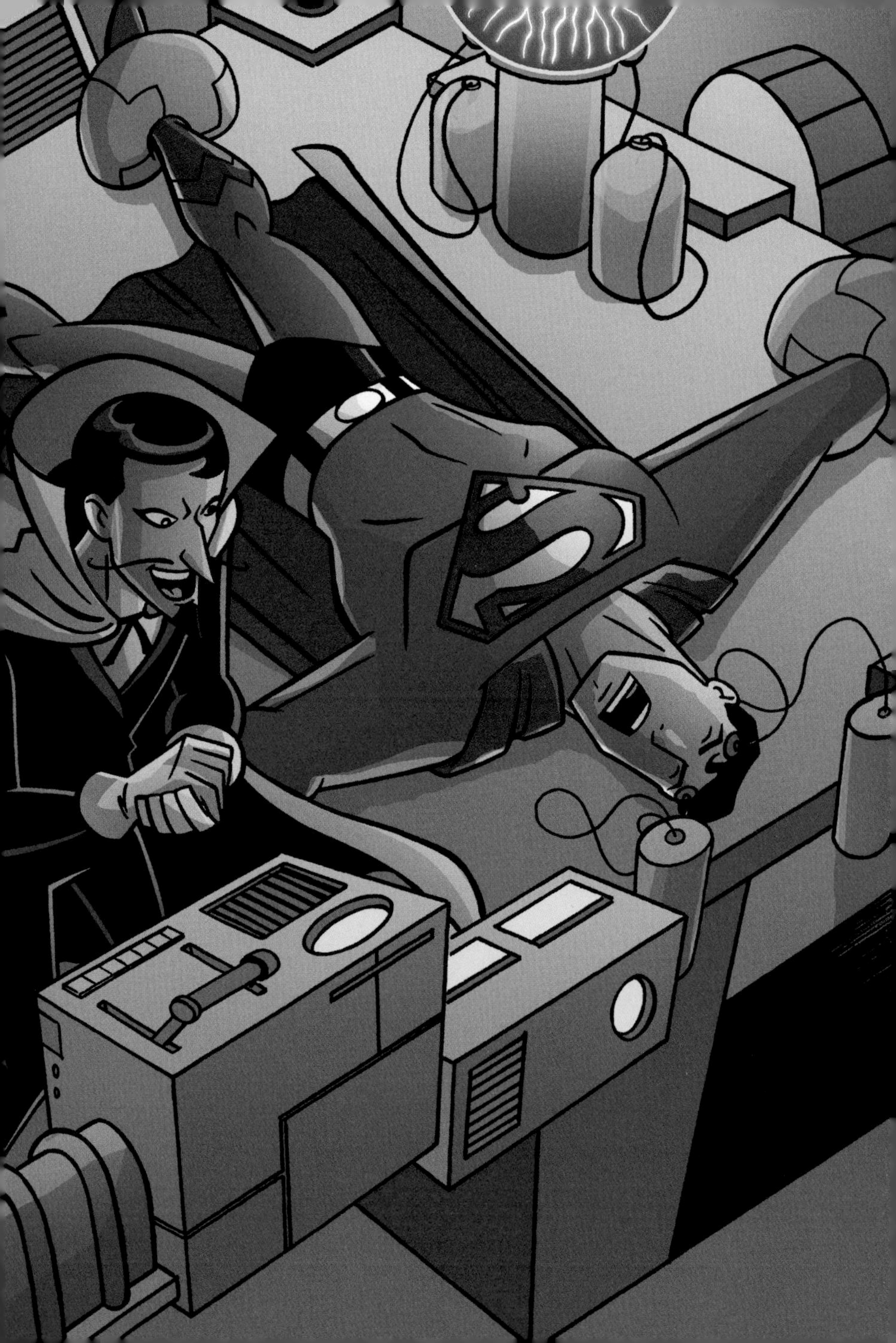

CHAPTER 2

UNBREAKABLE CHAINS

A few days earlier, Superman received a signal that an alien space shuttle had landed on Earth. The signal came from a stretch of the Mojave Desert in California.

Superman flew to the desert to check out the disturbance. From high in the air, he spotted the landing site and zoomed down to it. A man, more than six feet tall, stood by the shuttle. Despite the heat, the man wore a tuxedo. He had unpacked strange-looking technical equipment, which was placed around him on the sand.

"Superman," the man said, twirling his skinny moustache between his fingers. "I've been waiting for you."

Superman knew that the man's name was Abra Kadabra. He remembered the villain as a longtime enemy of the Flash. Superman had helped the Flash defeat Abra Kadabra in a few battles. The evil magician couldn't perform real magic, but since his technology in the 64th century was so advanced, it seemed like wizardry.

For the past few years, Abra Kadabra had been imprisoned on a distant planet called Salvation with other super-criminals. He had obviously managed to escape. Whatever Abra Kadabra was planning, Superman knew it couldn't be good.

"You're not welcome on Earth," Superman told the magician.

"I suggest you return to Salvation," the Man of Steel continued, "before I'm forced to take you back."

Abra Kadabra laughed. "I'm not going anywhere," he replied. "That's not why I escaped from Salvation."

"You've made your choice," Superman said. He rocketed toward Abra Kadabra. The Man of Steel swung a super-punch to flatten the villain.

ZHHINNGG!!

Superman's punch hit an invisible force field around Abra Kadabra. A silver box next to the villain made a loud whooshing noise. Then glowing, green energy burst out of the force field and rushed at Superman. The attack hit the super hero and knocked him dizzy.

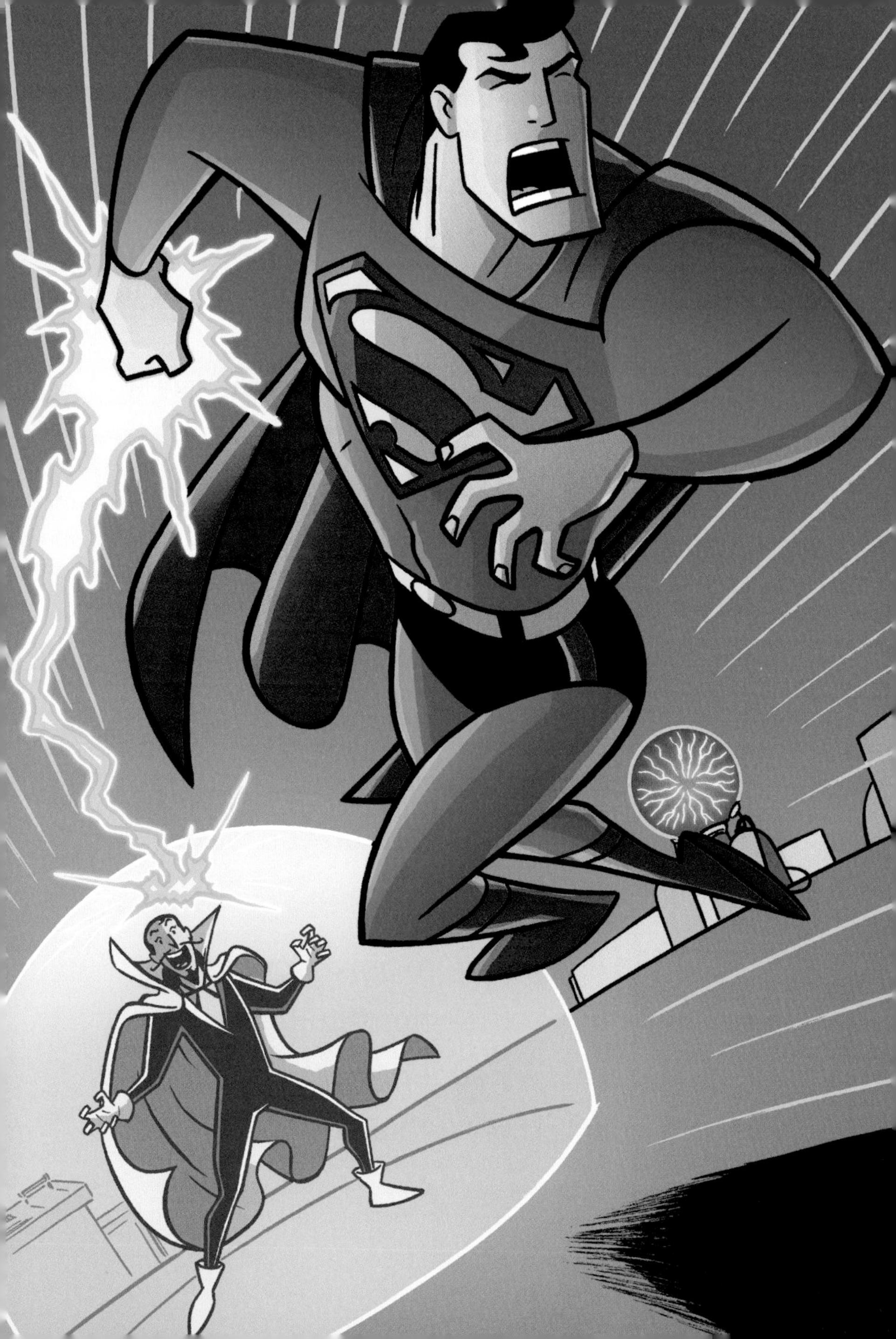

While Superman was still woozy, Abra Kadabra wrapped him up in sturdy chains that tingled with power.

When Superman's head cleared, he thrashed in the chains. **CHING! CLANK!** He was unable to free himself.

"Struggle all you want," Abra Kadabra said gleefully. "Like my force field, the chains absorb your own superpowers. The more you fight, the stronger they get. *You are the one powering them!*"

Superman stopped straining against the unbreakable chains. "What do you want from me?" he said with a groan.

"Before I escaped from Salvation, I learned about your relationship to Earth's yellow sun," Abra Kadabra replied. "I know you store solar power for energy."

Abra Kadabra pointed at a metal box nearby. The box started buzzing. **BZZT!**

Superman felt searing pain through his body. His energy was being drained by Abra Kadabra's technology.

"I'm using you as a giant solar battery," Abra Kadabra informed Superman. "I've created the most incredible machine. It can control the minds of everyone on this planet. The only problem is that it takes an insane amount of energy to power it. You're the only source strong enough!"

Abra Kadabra gestured to another machine. This one was a purple sphere that crackled with bolts of green lightning. "Now that you're connected to my machine," he said, "let's see if it works!" He closed his fist, and the machine started to glow.

The next thing Superman knew, he was Clark Kent, relaxing at the beach resort with Lois Lane. But when Lois had mentioned Superman's name, the super hero suddenly snapped out of the dream-like state. He knew the beach was an imaginary vision.

With his mind clear again, Superman looked around. Abra Kadabra had been busy while Superman was trapped in the dream. He had built a giant platform in the desert, with a huge electrical storage tank. A wireless electricity connection zapped power between Superman and the villain's machines. **BZZZT!**

A drip of water slid down the side of Superman's face. His super sense of smell caught a whiff of the drop. It was salty, with a hint of seaweed. Seawater!

His hair was wet from his imaginary swim with Lois. Somehow it was still damp in the real world.

Superman didn't know how that was possible, but it was certainly interesting.

Abra Kadabra was on the other side of the platform, constructing a tall antenna. While the villain was busy, Superman struggled against the cuffs. They didn't budge, but got stronger the more he used his super-strength.

Superman fixed his eyes on one of the thick handcuffs. He blasted it with his heat vision.

The cuff wasn't damaged at all! Abra Kadabra had coated the metal with lead, which blocked his heat vision.

"Awake, are we?" Abra Kadabra called, hurrying over to Superman's side.

"Your machine didn't work on me," Superman replied. "If you put me back into the dream, I'll break out again."

"It's a new technology," Abra Kadabra said. "There must be a bug in the system. Ah . . . did you remember who you were? That might pop you out."

Superman would not help Abra Kadabra by answering his question.

"I don't know what you're seeing in there," the villain explained. "At the moment, my machine makes you forget who you are and keeps you calm." He waved his hand, and the purple globe glowed. "There! I fixed the bug! Now people won't snap out of the dreams anymore."

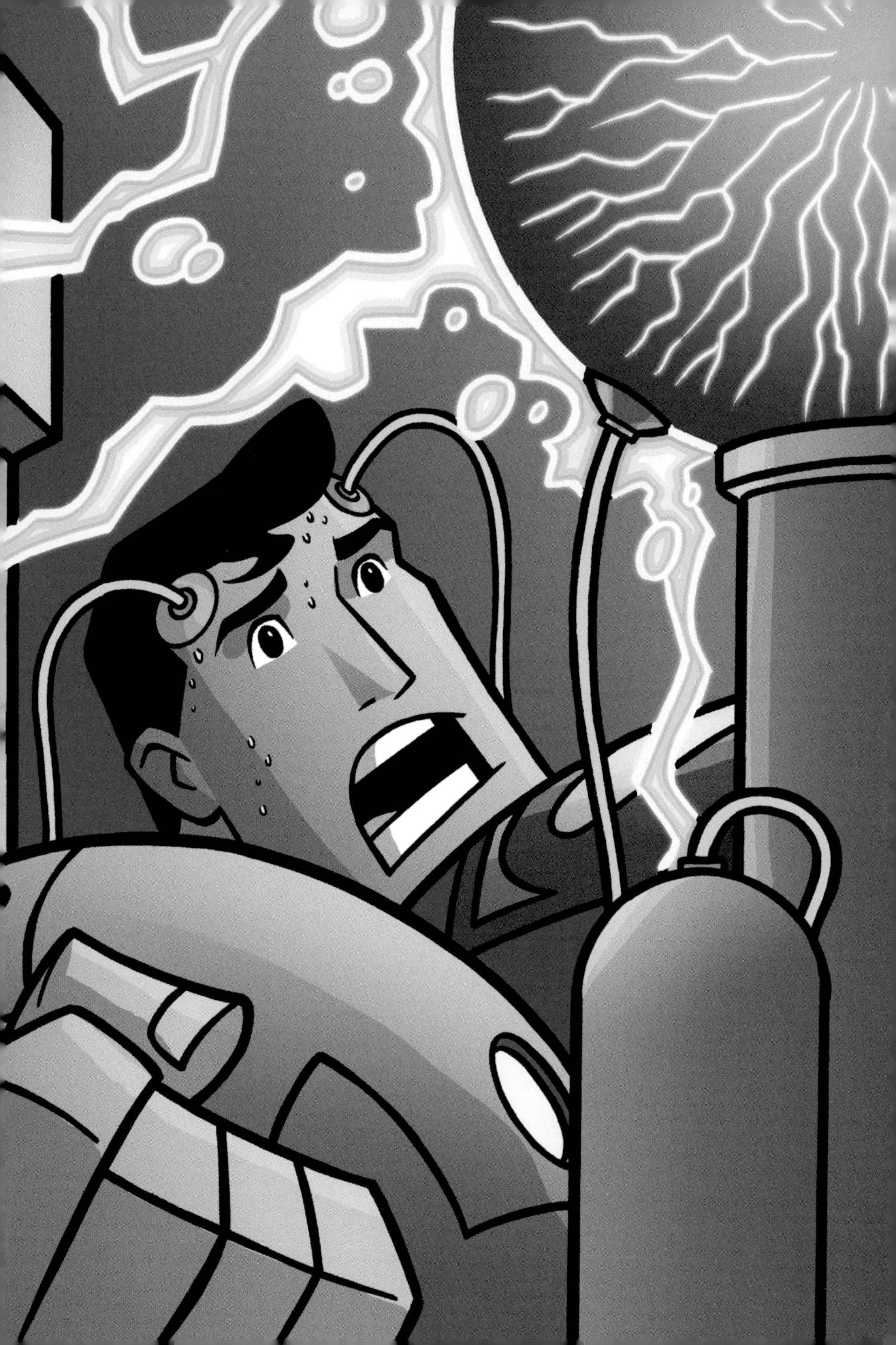

"I *will* break out," Superman swore.

"You *won't,*" Abra Kadabra replied. "Soon my machine will harness all of your power. Then I will brainwash everyone into believing that I am the world's High Sorcerer and adored rightful ruler of Earth. I'll also have the monopoly on a cheap and plentiful energy supply!"

Laughing, Abra Kadabra waved his hand again.

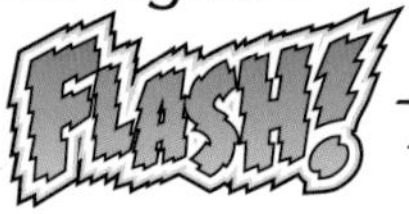
FLASH!
The purple globe flared with power.

CHAPTER 3

POWER OF IMAGINATION

Clark relaxed on the beach with Lois, soaking in the sun's rays.

"What a gorgeous beach," Lois said. She let out a sigh and put on her floppy hat.

"It's very peaceful," Clark replied.

There wasn't another person around. The only sound was the churn of the ocean. Behind them, past the dunes covered with sawgrass, palm trees quivered in the breeze. Near the trees, Clark spotted a white hotel shimmering in the hazy heat.

Something didn't feel right — it was too calm. "I feel . . . strange," Clark told Lois. "Maybe it's too peaceful."

"Don't be silly," Lois replied. "We deserve some peace, especially since we finished that big article on Superman for the *Daily Planet*."

Superman! thought Clark, sitting up straight. *How could I forget Superman? I am Superman!*

Clark remembered everything. He knew that he was being held prisoner in his own imagination by Abra Kadabra. His body was in the Mojave Desert, hooked up to the villain's machines. But remembering didn't snap him out of the vision this time.

"Lois, I don't think we're really here," Clark explained.

Lois laughed. "Of course we are," she said. "Where else would we be?"

"This may be a shock," Clark said. "I think I'm a prisoner in my own thoughts, which means you're probably imaginary."

"You know that sounds crazy, don't you, Clark?" she asked. "I don't feel imaginary."

"I know it's hard to believe," Clark replied. "I can prove it, though. Let's go check out the hotel."

"Why not?" Lois agreed. "We've seen some strange things over the years."

Clark and Lois hiked over the sand, pushing through the sharp sawgrass. The hotel shimmered as they got closer to the palm trees. When they reached the trees, the hotel disappeared, revealing more dunes covered with sawgrass.

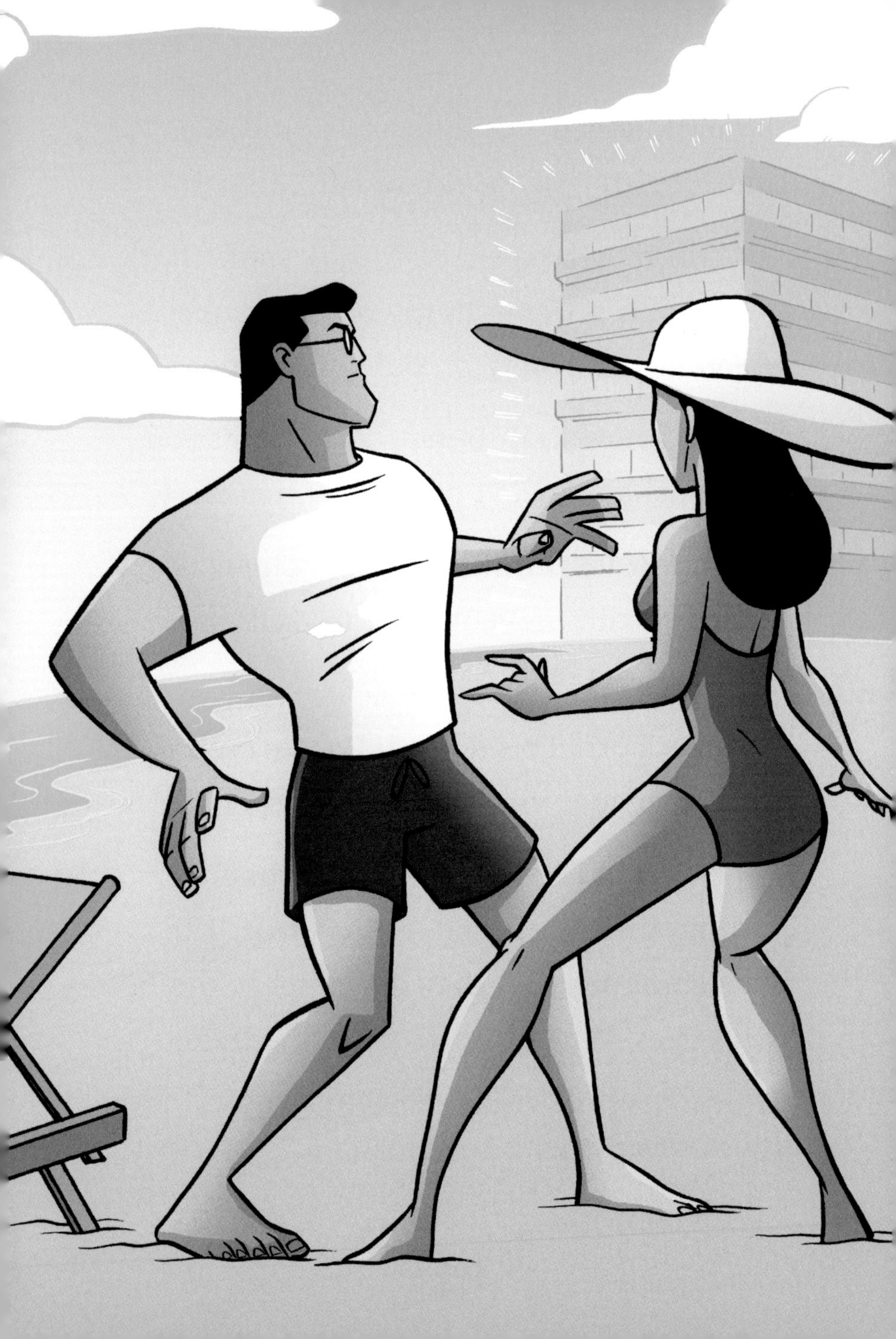

"The hotel was a mirage!" Clark said.

"That is surprising," Lois admitted, "but let's keep walking."

After a few steps across the dunes, the ocean appeared. When Clark and Lois reached the dune's peak, they saw their lounge chairs on the beach.

Clark followed Lois down to the chairs. They both sat, lost in thought.

"I know we didn't turn around," Lois said finally. "How did we end up where we started?"

"This beach resort isn't real, Lois," Clark said gently. "It's imaginary."

Lois nodded, dazed. "I'm adding up the facts," she admitted, "and you might be right. But . . . why are you a prisoner here?"

Whether in reality or in his imagination, Lois was the smartest person Clark knew. He needed her help to escape. This wasn't the real Lois Lane, so he could tell her the truth of his secret identity.

"I have another shock for you, Lois," Clark said softly. "I was captured by a villain named Abra Kadabra. He's keeping me here because . . . I'm Superman."

Lois gaped at him. Then she pulled herself together and smiled. "That makes so much sense!" she exclaimed. "Why didn't I put two and two together? I had my suspicions, because the two of you are never in the same place at the same time. You should have told me. You can trust me!"

"I'm trusting you now, Lois," Clark said. "I need your help."

"When I snapped out of the vision before," Clark continued, "my hair was still wet from swimming. So maybe what I do here affects my body in real life."

"Hmm," Lois began, thinking. "Can you fly here? Perhaps you can fly out of this dream."

"It's worth a shot," Clark replied. He leaped into the air and swooped above the beach chairs.

"You can!" Lois cheered. "Now fly fast enough to break out of here."

Clark soared down the beach. He picked up speed as he zoomed along the seashore. Soon, the Man of Steel was only a blur, flying faster than the speed of sound.

ZWWWOOOOMMMM!

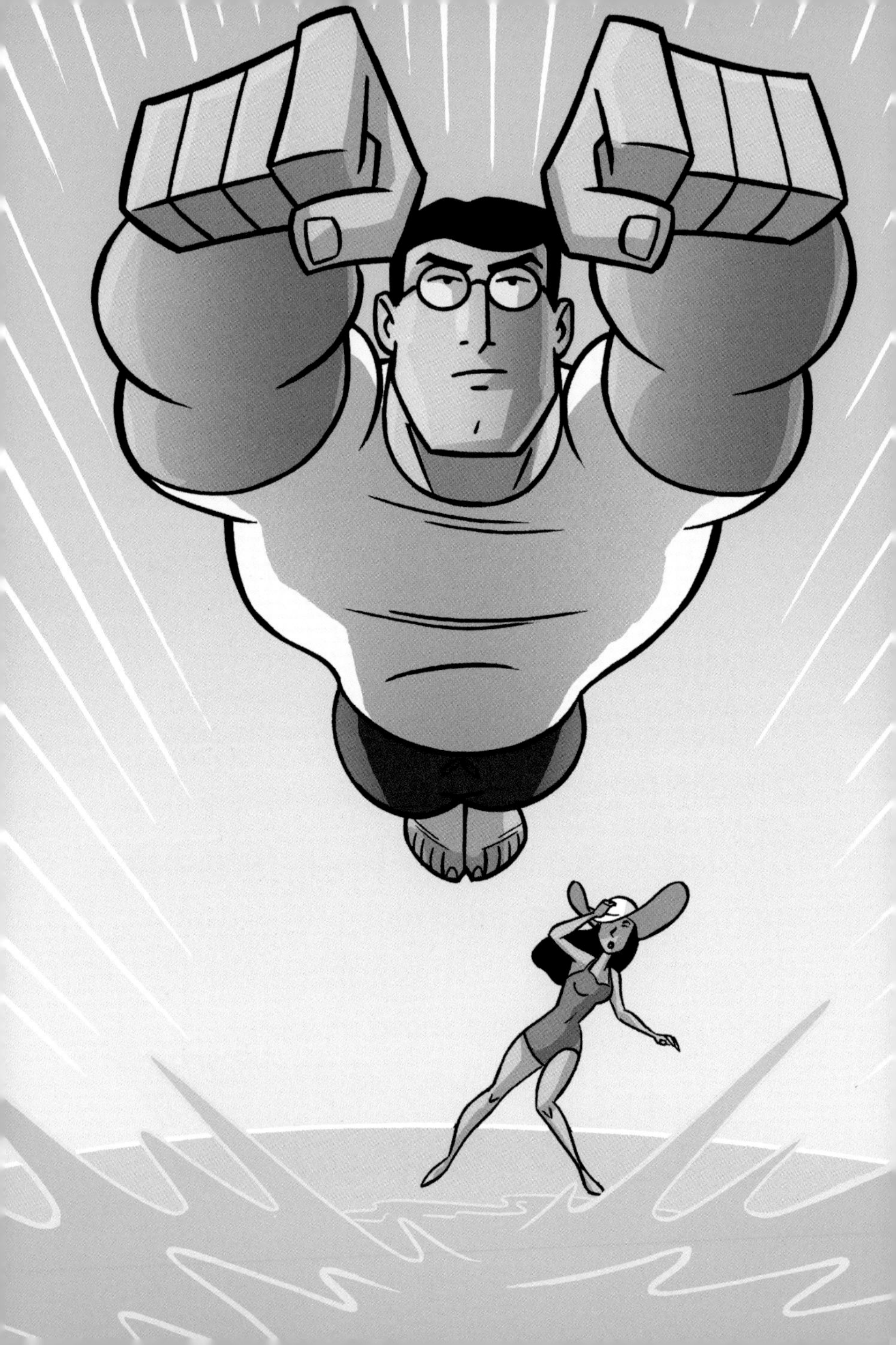

Then he spotted Lois and the beach chairs in front of him. Lois sat on the edge of her chair, staring in the other direction. He landed softly behind her.

"Lois," he said.

Lois screamed and whirled around. "Clark!" she scolded. "You startled me!"

"Sorry," he said, smiling. "Unfortunately, it's an endless loop of beach."

"All right," Lois said. "Let's tackle the problem from another direction. How does Abra Kadabra's machine work?"

Clark sat on his chair. "I get my superpowers from the sun," he explained. "Abra Kadabra's machines are running off my power as though I'm a solar battery."

"Interesting," Lois said. "So what happens when you're out of the sun?"

"Well," Clark replied, "I store the sun's energy for a long time. That's how I can fly through space to other solar systems. It's also why I don't get weaker at night."

Lois nodded her head. "Is it possible that if you were blocked from the sun for a long time, you might lose strength?" she asked, thinking out loud.

"It's possible," Clark said, "although I've never tried it."

"Abra Kadabra's technology is being powered by you," Lois continued. "If you're weak enough, his machines might turn off. You'd be free."

Clark stood up. "Let's give it a try," he said.

CHAPTER 4

DRAINING SUPERMAN

"We have to block all sunlight from reaching me," Clark said. "Is there sunscreen in your bag?"

Lois dug around in her beach bag. She pulled out a bottle and read the label. "SPF 40," she said. "That should help. Wrap the towels around yourself, too."

Clark covered himself in the sunscreen. Then he draped the towels over his body.

"One more thing," Lois said. She pulled off her hat and placed it on Clark's head.

"There," Lois said with a smile. "Don't you look cute!"

Lois sat back and waited. After a while, she asked, "Do you feel any weaker?"

"No," Clark replied. "It will take years this way. I've been charging with solar energy my entire life."

"We need a better way to weaken you," Lois said. "We can't just wait for your batteries to run down. If you exercise, will it drain your energy?"

"Good idea," Clark said. Keeping the hat on and the towels wrapped around him, Clark stood. He jumped up and down, waving his arms and legs, doing superpowered jumping jacks. Clark exercised so fast that his limbs blurred like a hummingbird's wings.

After an hour of jumping jacks, Clark stopped. "I feel a little weaker," he told Lois. "I'm not draining fast enough, though. I have to break out of this dream before Abra Kadabra finishes building his machine."

"Use your heat vision," Lois suggested. "That burns up a lot of energy, doesn't it?"

"Another good idea," Clark replied. He let loose a stream of heat vision into the ocean while he continued jumping jacks.

HISSSSSS

The water sizzled, evaporating where his heat vision hit it. It was a good thing this ocean was imaginary and endless!

After many hours of draining himself, Clark only felt about halfway drained. He stopped and sighed. "There has to be a way to make this go faster," he complained.

"Hmm," Lois said. "Well, maybe you're still getting too much sunlight. That would recharge you while you're trying to empty yourself. Even with SPF 40 and the towels and hat, some sunlight gets through."

Clark nodded. Then he smiled, struck with an idea. He spun around in place as fast as he could.

THWOOOOMMM!!

He drilled down into the sand, until only his head was showing. Clark stopped turning, and faced the ocean. He blasted the water with his heat vision again.

"You look funny," Lois said, laughing. "Just your head on the beach, shooting lasers out of your eyes. Wearing my hat!"

Clark smiled, but didn't stop firing his heat vision into the ocean.

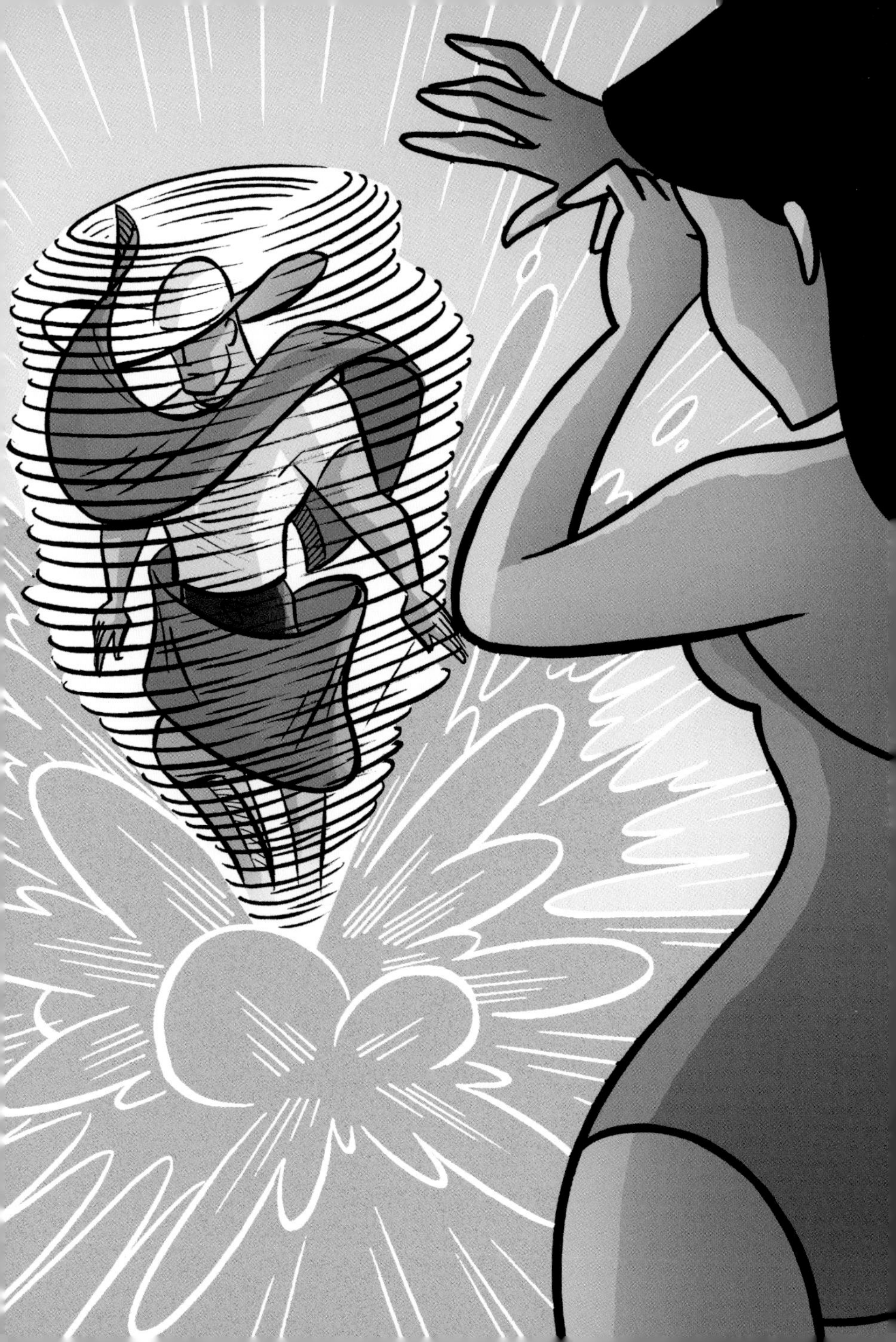

After many hours of waiting, Lois got bored. "Maybe there is such a thing as relaxing too much," she said. "I've lost track of time. Have days passed? It's hard to tell with no night." She let out a long sigh. "I wish I had a book to read."

"Maybe you do," Clark called to her. "Check your bag."

Lois opened her beach bag. In the bottom of the bag, she found a thick paperback detective novel. "That's perfect!" she cheered. "I wanted to read this."

"Read it out loud," Clark said. "Shooting endless heat vision beams is boring."

Lois settled into her chair. "It's a good thing we don't have to eat in your dream," she told Clark. "I don't feel like fishing for whatever creatures are in that ocean!"

"There's no life in there at all," Clark replied. "Except seaweed."

"Well," Lois said, "if I have to be part of a dream, I'm glad I get to spend time on a beautiful beach with you, Clark." She opened the book to the first page. "I'm rather enjoying being imaginary."

Then Lois read her book aloud. By the time Lois reached chapter six, Clark's heat vision was much weaker.

When Lois finally read the last page, the bolts of energy had fizzled to nothing.

Clark was empty.

The beach around Clark shimmered. He turned his head to glance at Lois. She looked transparent. He could see the palm trees through her body.

The vision vanished.

CHAPTER 5

SOLAR POWER

Superman was on the smooth metal platform, surrounded by Abra Kadabra's technological equipment. The machine was nearly complete. He had to act fast before the blazing sun of the Mojave desert powered him up again.

The purple sphere was calm, with no green lightning inside it. The hum of the cuffs binding him had fallen silent. The gadgets no longer had his superpowers to fuel them. Superman slipped the restraints off his body and fell to his knees. *THUD!*

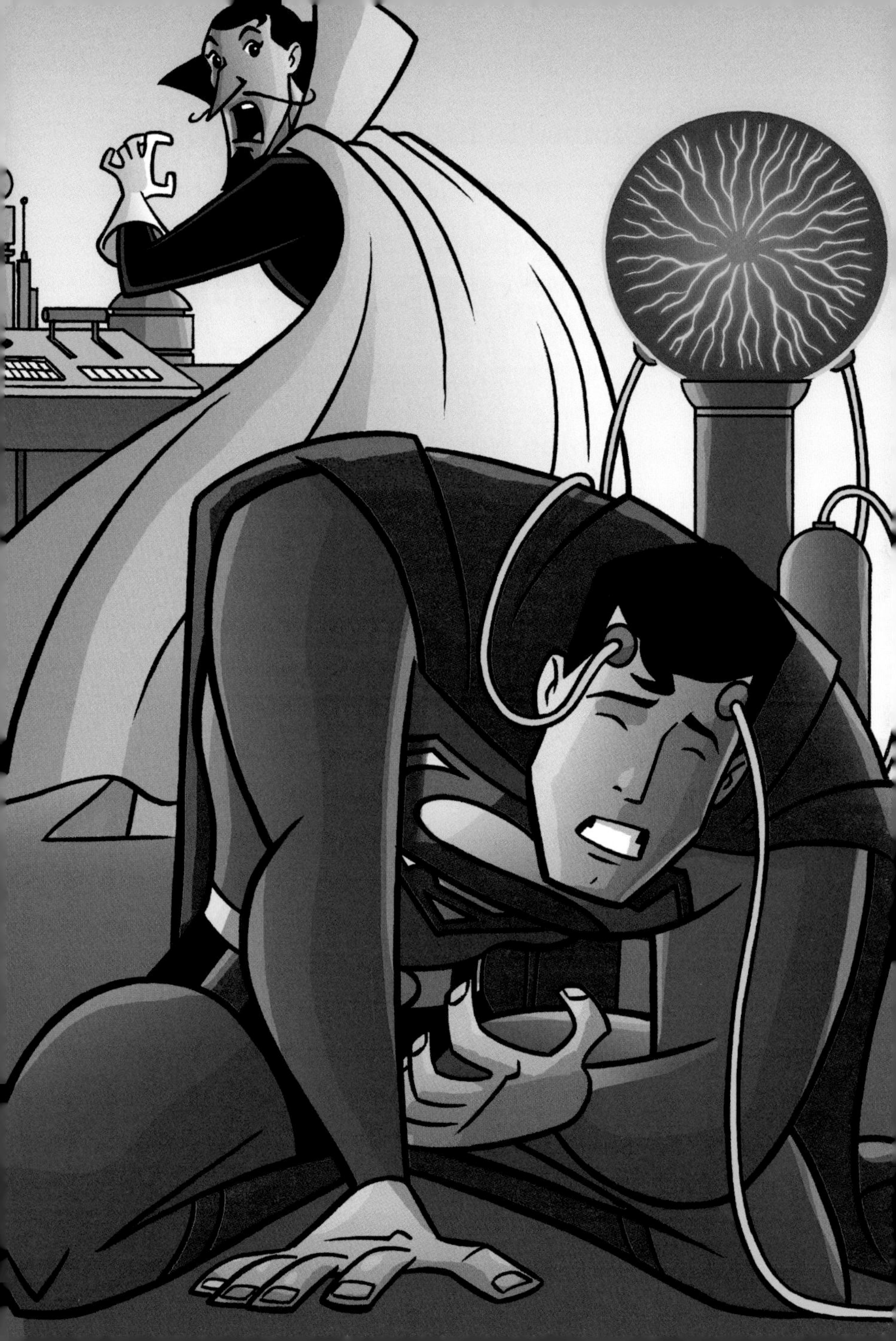

As he climbed to his feet, he felt terribly weak. Superman wondered if this was how normal men with no superpowers felt.

Suddenly, an alarm shrieked, signaling that the machine was losing power. Abra Kadabra bolted across the platform. "How did you get out?" he screamed.

"Maybe this 'S' on my chest stands for surprise," Superman replied. He fired his heat vision at Abra Kadabra. **FzzzT!** His eyes simply glowed and flickered. He wasn't used to fighting without his powers!

"You can't stop me!" Abra Kadabra shouted. "You can't touch me with your superpowers. Once I figure out what's wrong with my machine, you'll be back in that dream — forever!"

Superman walked toward Abra Kadabra on his shaky legs. The villain didn't back away, secure in his force field. Superman was counting on that happening.

When he was close enough, Superman clasped his hands together. He swung his fists with all his might.

Abra Kadabra didn't even duck.

WHAAAMMMMMM!

The blow hit the villain squarely on the side of his head. Abra Kadabra crumpled to the floor, knocked out.

"I don't have superpowers right now," Superman told the unconscious villain. "And your force field doesn't protect against a punch from a *normal* man!"

While Abra Kadabra was knocked out, Superman dragged him off the platform.

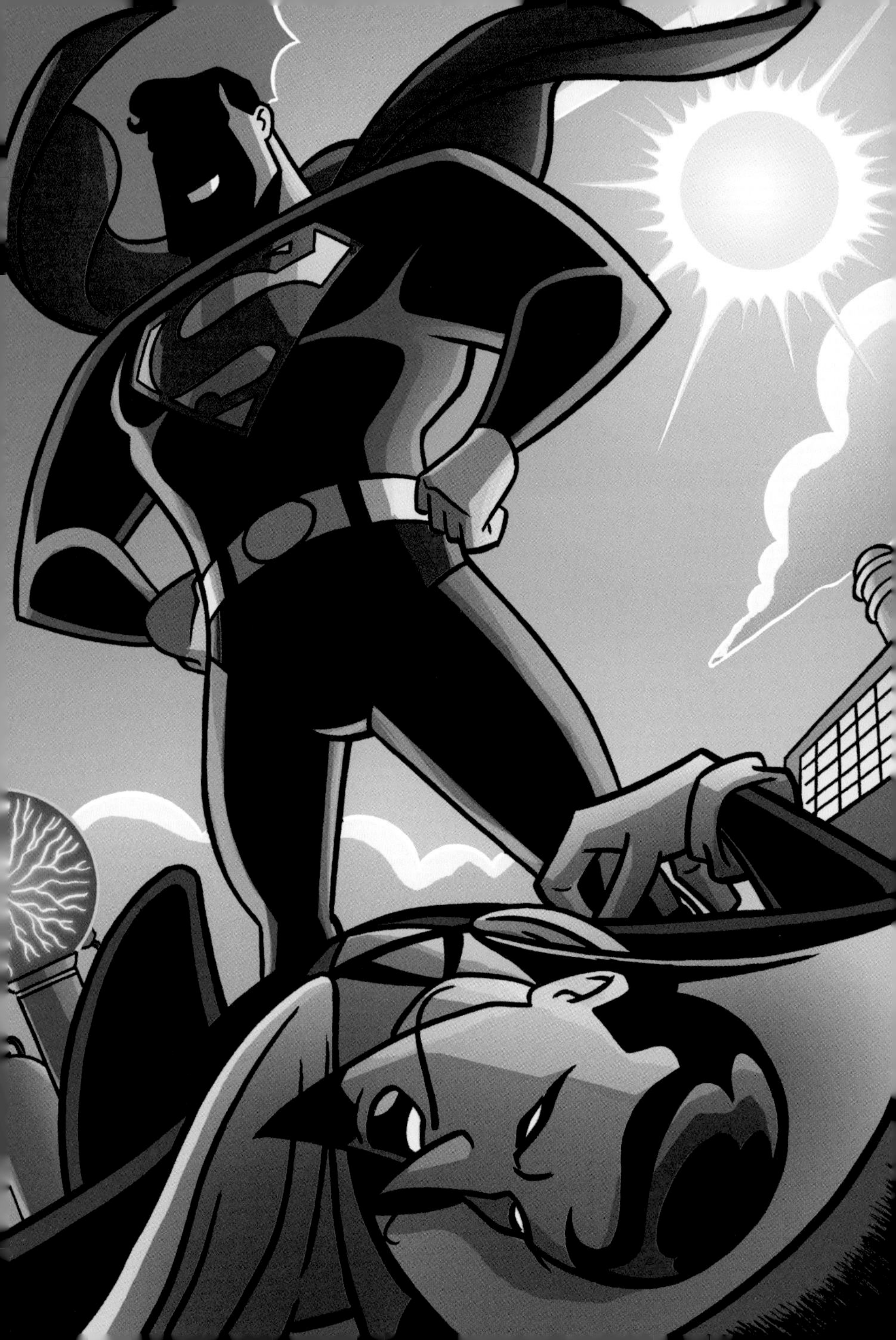

The Man of Steel was surprised how heavy the villain seemed, but the sunlight was already powering Superman back up.

He pulled Abra Kadabra to his shuttle. After stuffing the villain inside the small spacecraft, Superman programmed the controls and locked Abra Kadabra inside.

Then Superman raised his face to the sun and held out his arms. He drank in the pure power of the yellow star. There were no clouds to filter the light. The energy surging into Superman's body felt amazing.

When Superman had recharged enough, he returned to the shuttle. Abra Kadabra was waking up inside.

Superman picked up the spacecraft.

"Wait!" Abra Kadabra yelled. "Don't send me back!"

"This is what's in my power to give you," Superman replied. He cocked his arm.

THWOOOOMMMMMM!!

With a mighty heave, Superman launched the shuttle out of the Earth's atmosphere. It was programmed to take Abra Kadabra directly back to Salvation.

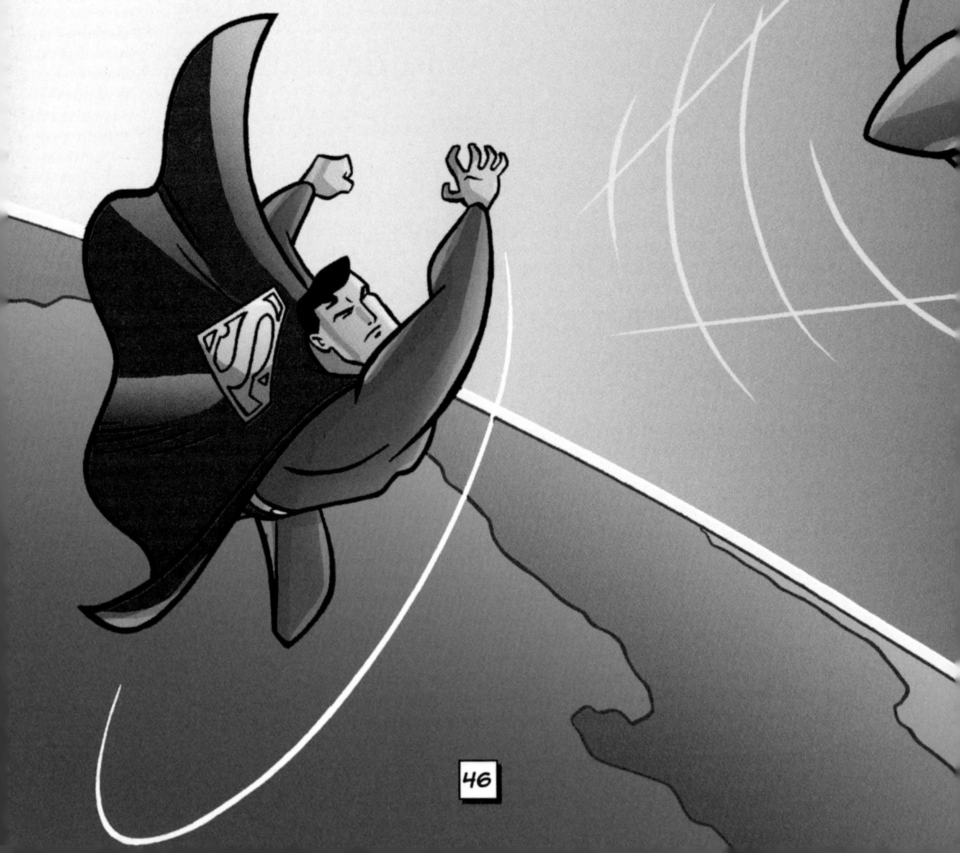

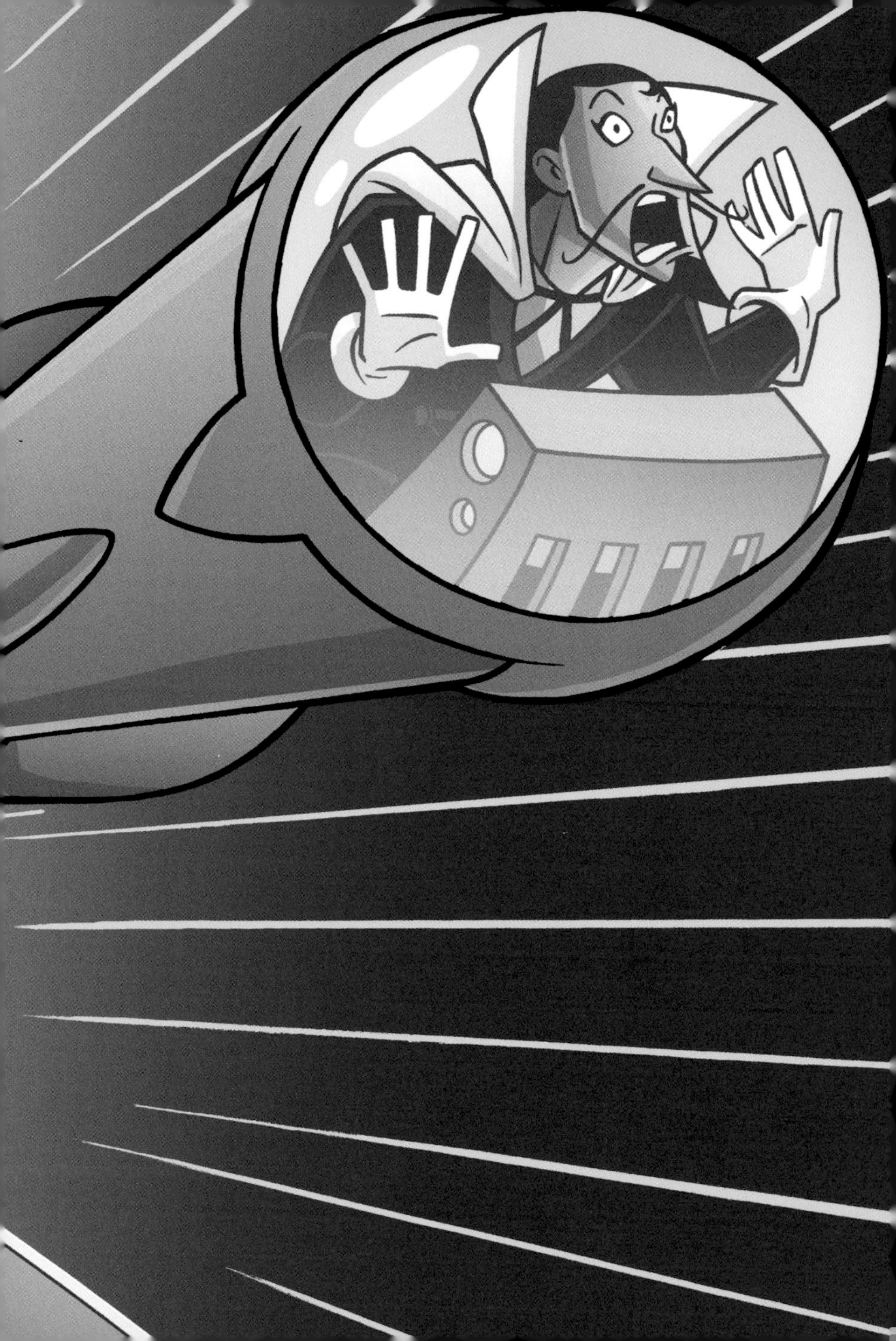

Superman heaved a sigh of relief. Throwing the spacecraft through the atmosphere had used the last of his super-strength. He collapsed on the platform and soaked in the sun's yellow rays.

After a few hours, he felt recharged enough to pick up the whole platform and the machines attached to it. He tossed all the equipment out of Earth's atmosphere. He sent the evil technology on a collision course into the sun.

*   *   *

The next day, Clark visited Lois Lane at her desk in the Daily Planet offices.

"Um, hi, Lois," he said awkwardly. "Have you read any good detective novels lately?"

Lois blinked at him. "Detective novels?" she asked. "Clark, have you lost your mind? I wish I had time to read detective novels. I'm too busy working on a story about solar power. Did you know that the real problem is finding a good way to store the electricity generated?"

Clark laughed. "Yes, I heard about that," he replied. "Writing about solar energy is a great idea, Lois. Solar power can be very useful!"

Lois shook her head. "You're goofier than usual today, Clark," she said.

"Sorry," Clark replied. "I'm just a little drained today."

Lois sighed. "Maybe we should *both* take a vacation," she suggested.

Clark smiled. "Anywhere but the beach!"

DAILY PLANET

FROM THE DESK OF CLARK KENT

WHO IS ABRA KADABRA?

Abra Kadabra is a magician who once lived in the 64th century. In that time, technology was so advanced that Abra's magic tricks seemed silly in comparison. No one attended his performances, and the magician was soon out of a job. So Kadabra stole some of his era's technology and used it to travel backward in time to the 21st century! Now, in the present day, he uses his powers in an attempt at world domination. Only Superman, the Man of Tomorrow, stands in the way of this time traveler's evil plans.

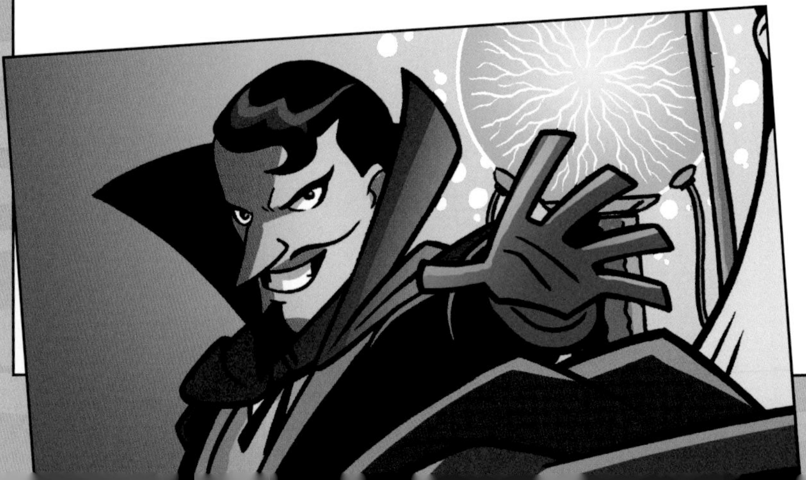

- Abra Kadabra's costume has a seemingly harmless flower. However, this piece of jewelry is anything but ordinary — Abra's Hypno-Ray can brainwash anyone, including even the Man of Steel himself!

- Abra Kadabra got his super-villain nickname from the phrase "Abracadabra," a word used by many of today's magicians. In the Aramaic language, the word "Abracadabra" means "I will create as I speak," making the word a perfect name for a magician who casts spells.

- Abra Kadabra grew jealous when the Flash became popular. He turned the super hero speedster into a living puppet! Abra Kadabra used the animatronic super hero in his live magic performances until the Flash managed to break free of the magician's clever spell.

BIOGRAPHIES

J.E. Bright has had more than 50 novels, novelizations, and non-fiction books published for children and young adults. He is a full-time freelance writer, living in a tiny apartment in the SoHo neighborhood of Manhattan with his good, fat cat, Gladys, and his evil cat, Mabel, who is getting fatter.

Gregg Schigiel is originally from South Florida. He knew he wanted to be a cartoonist since he was 11 years old. He's worked on projects featuring Batman, Spider-Man, SpongeBob SquarePants, and just about everything in between. Gregg currently lives and works in New York City.

Lee Loughridge Lee Loughridge has been working in comics for more than fifteen years. He currently lives in sunny California in a tent on the beach.

GLOSSARY

atmosphere (AT-muhss-feer)—the mixture of gases that surrounds a planet

barren (ba-RUHN)—unable to support growth, or empty and lifeless

brainwash (BRAYN-wahsh)—to make someone accept and believe something by repeating it over and over again

harness (HAR-niss)—to control and use something

massive (MASS-iv)—large, heavy, and solid

mirage (muh-RAZH)—something that you think you can see in the distance, like water in a desert, that is not actually there

monopoly (muh-NOP-uh-lee)—complete control of something

shimmered (SHIM-urd)—shined with unsteady light

transparent (transs-PAIR-uhnt)—clear like glass, or light can shine through

wizardry (WIZ-urd-ree)—magic

DISCUSSION QUESTIONS

1. Abra Kadabra uses magic to fight Superman. Do you believe in magic? Why or why not?

2. Which powers are better — Abra Kadabra's magical powers or Superman's superpowers? Whose powers would you rather have?

3. Some people believe dreams have hidden meaning. What do you think?

WRITING PROMPTS

1. Superman has a dream that he thinks is real. What kinds of dreams have you had? Write about your dreams.

2. The Man of Steel is a super hero. If you were a super hero, what would you look like? What would you do with your new powers? Write about your adventures as a super hero.

3. Abra Kadabra invented a machine that could steal Superman's strength. Create your own invention. What does it do? How does it look? Write about your creation, and then draw a picture of it.

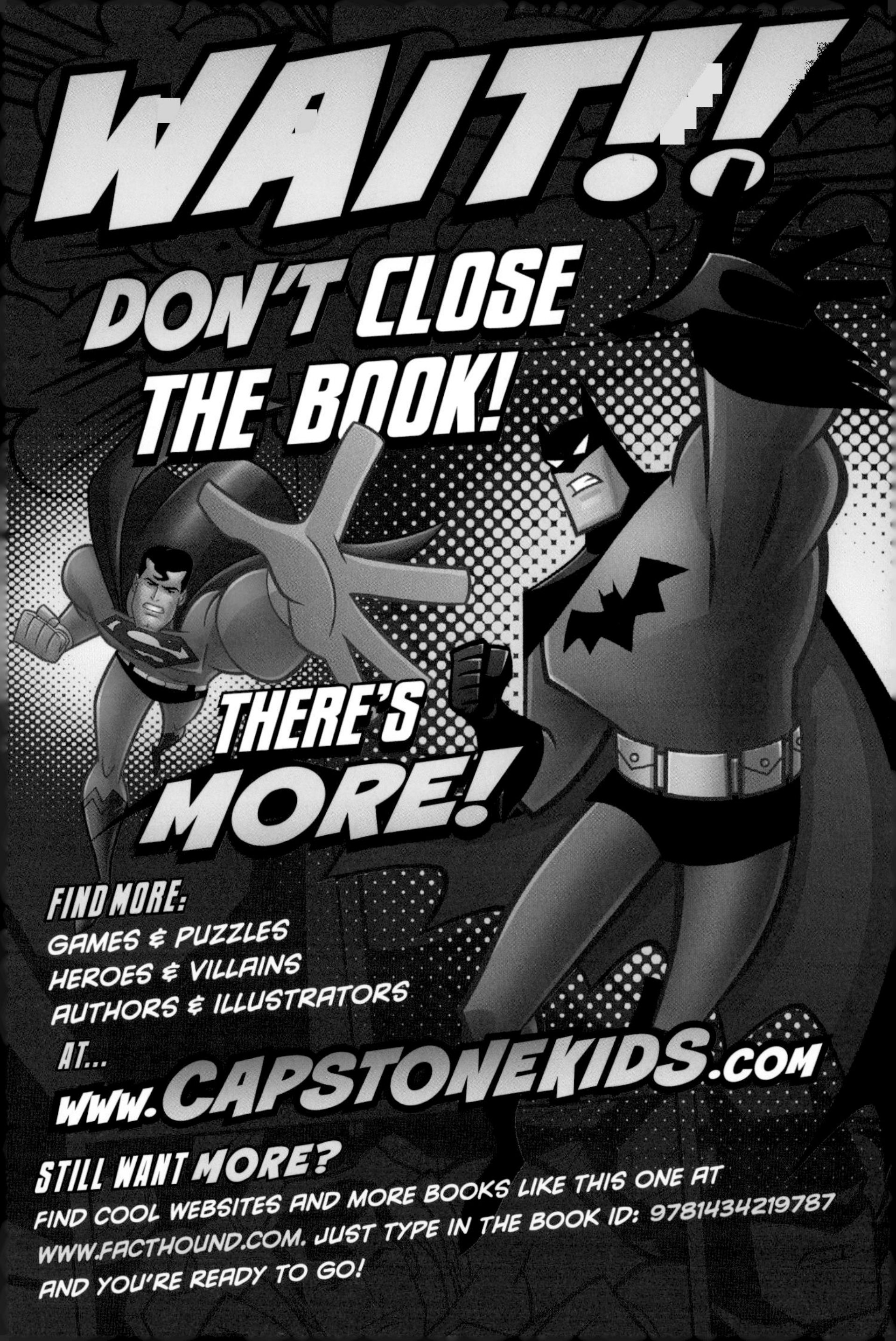
WAIT!!
DON'T CLOSE THE BOOK!
THERE'S MORE!
FIND MORE:
GAMES & PUZZLES
HEROES & VILLAINS
AUTHORS & ILLUSTRATORS
AT...
WWW.CAPSTONEKIDS.COM
STILL WANT MORE?
FIND COOL WEBSITES AND MORE BOOKS LIKE THIS ONE AT WWW.FACTHOUND.COM. JUST TYPE IN THE BOOK ID: 9781434219787 AND YOU'RE READY TO GO!

MORE NEW
SUPERMAN
ADVENTURES!

COSMIC BOUNTY HUNTER

DEEP SPACE HIJACK

PRANKSTER OF PRIME TIME

THE DEADLY DOUBLE

THE SHADOW MASTERS

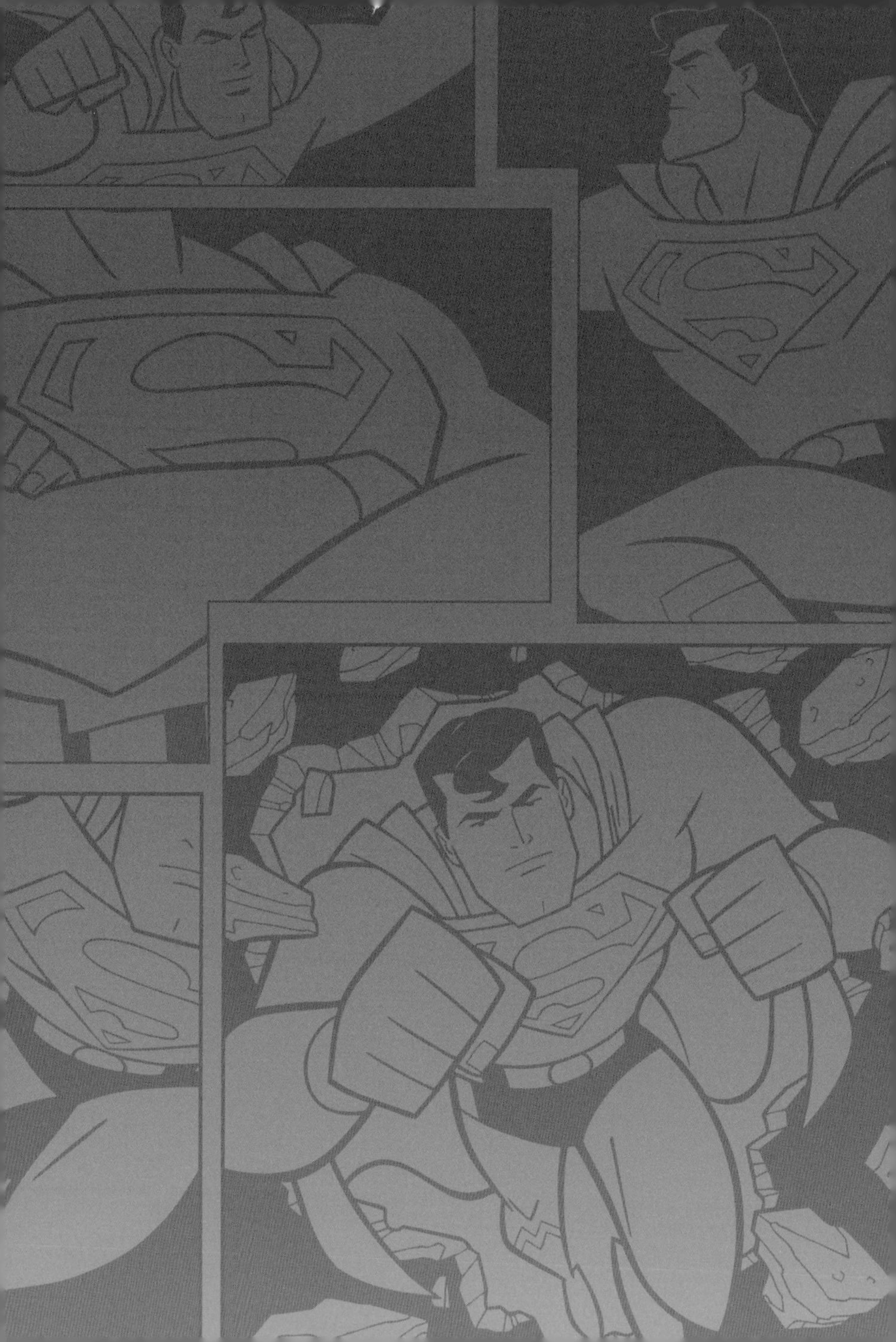

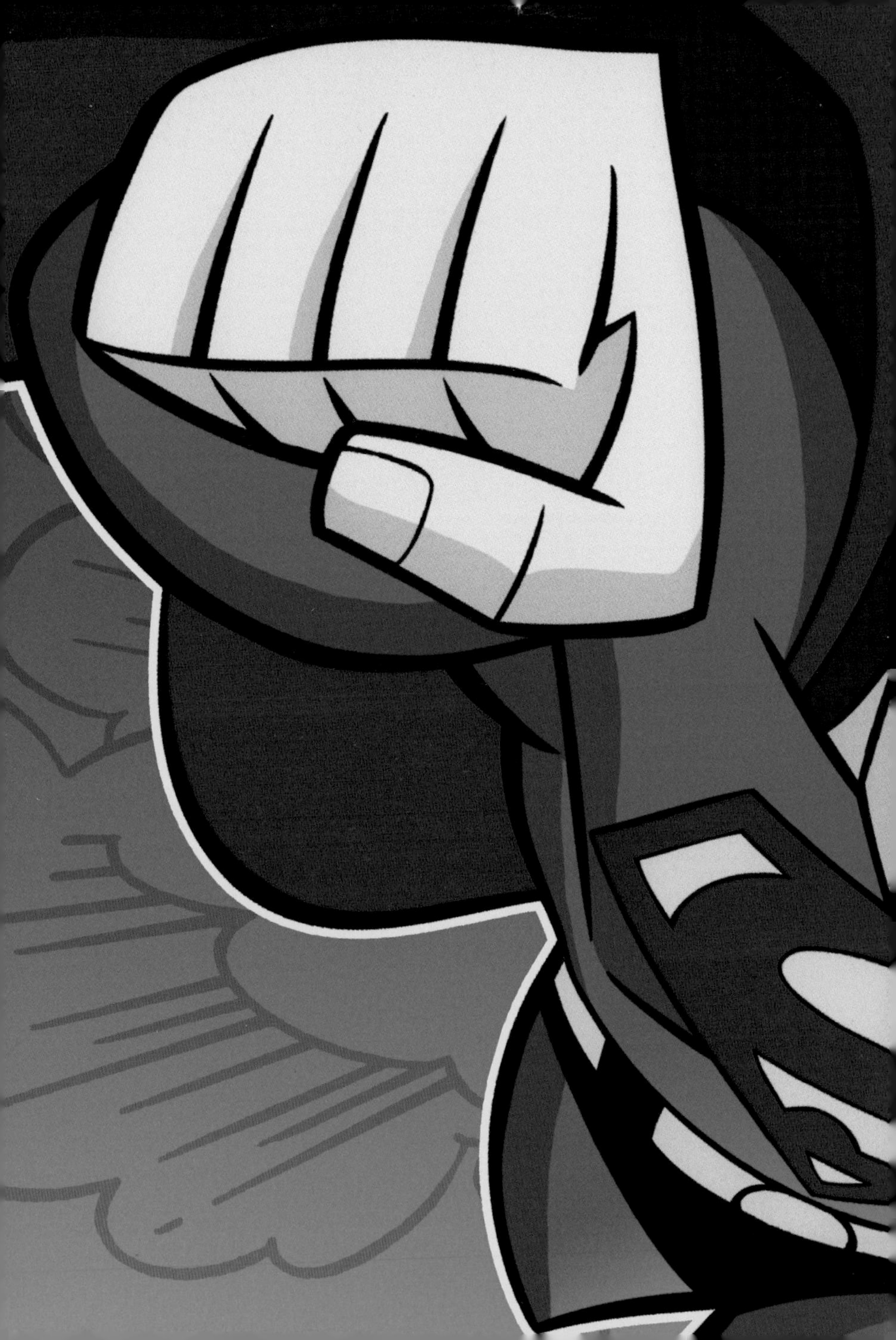